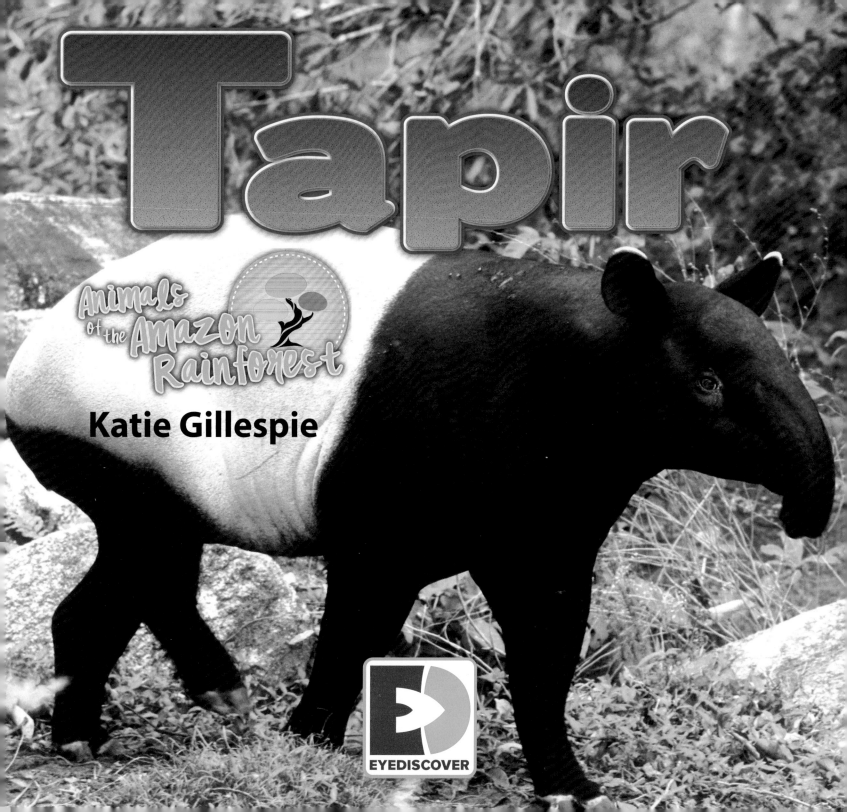

Tapir

Animals of the Amazon Rainforest

Katie Gillespie

EYEDISCOVER

EYEDISCOVER

Go to **www.eyediscover.com** and enter this book's unique code.

BOOK CODE

U755233

EYEDISCOVER brings you optic readalongs that support active learning.

Published by AV² by Weigl
350 5th Avenue, 59th Floor   New York, NY   10118
Website: www.eyediscover.com

Library of Congress Control Number: 2016938327

ISBN 978-1-4896-4573-9 (hardcover)

Printed in the United States of America
in Brainerd, Minnesota
1 2 3 4 5 6 7 8 9 0   20 19 18 17 16

042016
041516

Editor: Katie Gillespie
Designer: Mandy Christiansen

Weigl acknowledges Getty Images, Alamy, and Shutterstock as the primary image suppliers for this title.

EYEDISCOVER provides enriched content, optimized for tablet use, that supplements and complements this book. EYEDISCOVER books strive to create inspired learning and engage young minds in a total learning experience.

I am a lion.

Watch
Video content brings each page to life.

Browse
Thumbnails make navigation simple.

Read
Follow along with text on the screen.

Listen
Hear each page read aloud.

Your EYEDISCOVER Optic Readalongs come alive with...

Audio
Listen to the entire book read aloud.

Video
High resolution videos turn each spread into an optic readalong.

OPTIMIZED FOR

☑ **TABLETS**

☑ **WHITEBOARDS**

☑ **COMPUTERS**

☑ **AND MUCH MORE!**

Tapir

In this book, you will learn about

- **how I look**
- **where I live**
- **what I eat**

and much more!

5

I am a large animal with bristly dark hair. I have small eyes and short, round ears.

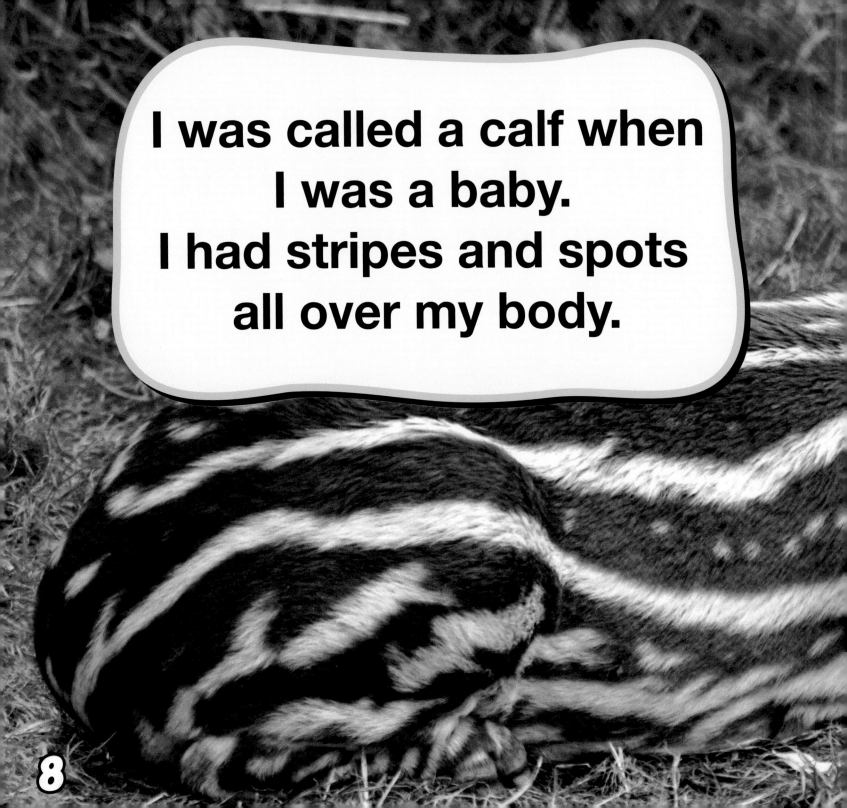

I was called a calf when I was a baby.
I had stripes and spots all over my body.

8

9

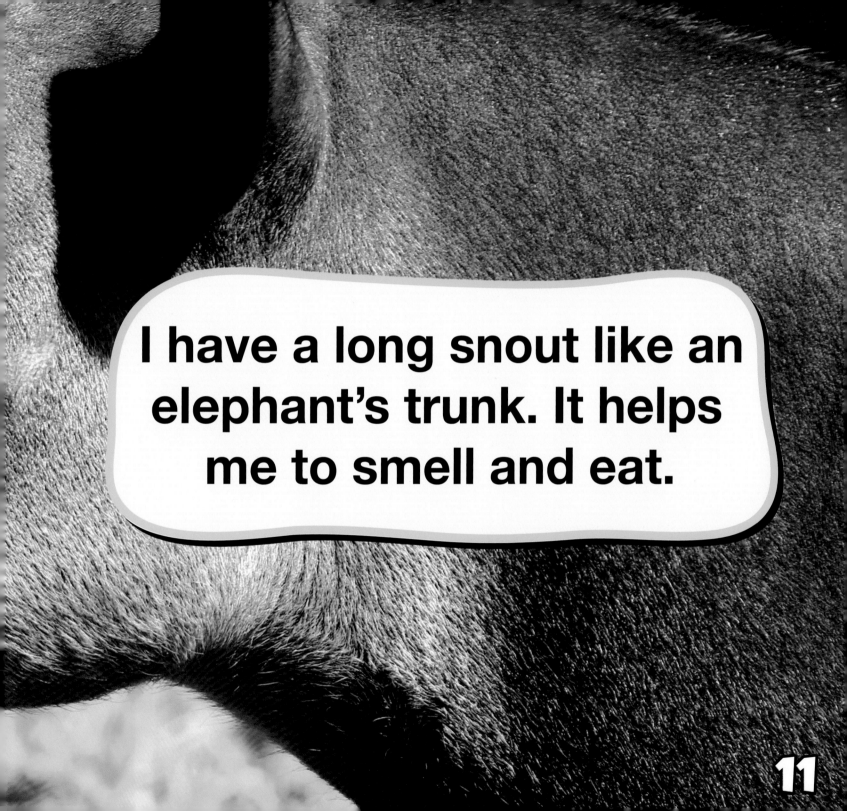

I have a long snout like an elephant's trunk. It helps me to smell and eat.

13

I eat many different kinds of plants. Leaves are my favorite meal.

15

I love to be in the water. I am very good at swimming.

19

21

TAPIRS BY THE NUMBERS

Tapirs can use their **snout** like a **snorkel** in the water.

Tapirs have lived on Earth for **20** million years.

There were tapirs living in **Southern California** about **10,000** years ago.

Tapirs are **related** to horses and rhinos.

A **group** of tapirs is called a **candle**.

Tapirs can make a **whistling sound** like screeching **car brakes.**

There are **5** different species of **tapirs**.

KEY WORDS

Research has shown that as much as 65 percent of all written material published in English is made up of 300 words. These 300 words cannot be taught using pictures or learned by sounding them out. They must be recognized by sight. This book contains 50 common sight words to help young readers improve their reading fluency and comprehension. This book also teaches young readers several important content words, such as proper nouns. These words are paired with pictures to aid in learning and improve understanding.

Page	Sight Words First Appearance
4	a, am, I
7	and, animal, eyes, have, large, small, with
8	all, had, my, over, was, when
11	an, eat, helps, it, like, long, me, to
12	food, for, most, of, time
14	are, different, kinds, leaves, many, plants
16	at, be, good, in, the, very, water
19	can, keep, this, under
20	home, near, need, trees

Page	Content Words First Appearance
4	tapir
7	ears, hair
8	baby, body, calf, spots, stripes
11	snout, trunk
14	meal

I am a lion.

Watch
Video content brings each page to life.

Browse
Thumbnails make navigation simple.

Read
Follow along with text on the screen.

Listen
Hear each page read aloud.

EYEDISCOVER

Go to www.eyediscover.com and enter this book's unique code.

BOOK CODE

U 7 5 5 2 3 3